MATING IN
CAPTIVITY

For Brian
love
Olivia

6/13/94

MATING IN CAPTIVITY

GENNI GUNN

QUARRY
PRESS

The author would like to thank Carolyn Smart for her editorial advice, Marven Donati for her artwork, and Bob Hilderley for his continuing support. Some of these poems have previously appeared in *And Other Travels*, *CCLow*, *Contemporary Verse 2*, *The Fiddlehead*, *The New Quarterly*, *Poetry Canada*, and *Quarry Magazine*.

The publisher gratefully acknowledges the assistance of The Canada Council, the Ontario Arts Council, the Department of Communications, and the Ontario Publishing Centre.

Canadian Cataloguing in Publication Data

Gunn, Genni, 1949 —
    Mating in captivity

Poems.
ISBN 1–55082– 067–2

    I. Title.

PS8563.U572M38 1993   C811'.54   C93
PR9199.3.G86M38   1993

Cover art by Marven Donati, reproduced by permission of the artist. Design by Keith Abraham. Typeset by Susan Hannah. Printed and bound in Canada by Best-Gagné Book Manufacturers, Toronto, Ontario.

Published by Quarry Press, Inc., P.O. Box 1061, Kingston, Ontario K7L 4Y5.

CONTENTS

NATURAL
HABITATS

VARIATIONS OF SILENCE

It's what you carry with you whenever you move from one decisive space to another; the essence of treasures your mother gives you one day when you are no longer a child: your first doll and a packet of letters written to your father when you were four. She has kept the doll, she tells you, because she can recall the moment you unwrapped it, the delight on your face, your thin arms cradling. Womanhood, she says. But you don't recall that particular moment. The doll, with her hard straw body and splintered porcelain crown, has eyes which shut each time her head inclines. This image you carry into strange beds with lovers and husbands. Your mother insists you loved that doll and cried when her head split open, but you remember a small sacrifice — a quick blow on cement, three pieces of jagged porcelain — to uncover the mystery behind the eyes. And all these years, that metal arm has weighed your lids shut.

It's what you seek when you scale the steps and emerge, years later, in an attic scorched with summer, the stifling heat of Italy in August when cities empty to stone tombs and seasides fill with the shrieks of children. Displacements. Water poured glass to glass. Diminishing returns. Your imprints fade. In the packet of letters a scream is tightly wound within the shape of words dictated by an aunt in a foreign tongue. *Dear Daddy, How are you? I am fine.* You slide the elastic carefully over the envelopes and blue wings cascade into your hands. The words flutter across an ocean. You imagine your father capturing them decades ago, bewildered perhaps, by the reminder of a strange little girl he rarely sees. And you, perhaps, bewildered by children whose fathers are near, whose love is noisy and contagious. It's not the letters, or the meaning, or the act of writing you recall, but the moment, years later, when you discover he has kept them all. It's this surprise you recognize in lovers and husbands who can't say the words any more than you can or could when your father was alive. And you respond to their metal arms, and fan your wings to ignite straw hearts.

It's the response to the letter your long-term lover sends, asking you to come. You never write him back, but always take the next plane out — two connections — and arrive in Las Vegas late evening when you can almost believe the crescent moon is man's invention, as night glitters in neon, a concrete sculpture of water and fire. You take a taxi to his hotel. He is a permanent transient here, on rest-stops between gold mines he prospects in the hills, states, and provinces of a continent, as if borders don't exist. But you know they do, those personal borders you can never cross. The wedge between you, a silent accusation you have felt him hammering since you were twenty, when he returned from a six-month absence, and found you gone. This failure you have worn like a shield against men. Each time you leave, you understand that history is cyclical, and fate inevitable, like watching the same movie to the same end.

It's what you read between the lines of his letters: the void no husbands and wives and lovers can fill. His life shaped by your entrances and exits; your life shaped by his needs and denials. And you reply by being there, and spend your days with him by a riverbed, upturning stones, as if you can unearth the past, reroute the blood which flows in thin veins underneath. Fools' gold.

It's how your lover beckons on a winter day as you walk the shore of a crescent beach. His need, the whimper of a familiar stray slithering in the caves between rocks, bones protruding, eyes wild. He claws windows in your heart, then crawls in. But you know all along that he belongs elsewhere, in a house with a wife, a son, a life you can't imagine. Only words. Their presence, a foreign language he returns to, rough and familiar as a mother's tongue licking her young while feeding.

It's what you feel in his embrace the first time, the loss of words. Visual dialogue — his eyes, your eyes — as your fingers slide along his ribs. Like falling down stairs or waking with a sudden jolt from a flying dream seconds before hitting ground. Or when he calls, aphonia, the loss of voice. He articulates only the impossible, a sequence of uncertainties which haunt you month to month while you slide slowly into languor. Unnamed, the space between you grows, and hours crawl between visits. The flicker of digital clocks, a neon displacement of time and place. Reds, greens, halt, begin. Armed with electrical tape and scissors, you cover each until there is total darkness, and wear black to absorb absence.

It's what you see in all the plants that hunch, unwatered, on the sill, months later, when he no longer calls. Unable to utter sound, mouths open for quenching.

It's the ache, the loneliness after an evening out with your women friends. Excruciating hours, when you lie in darkness, exhausted, and can't sleep because you need to hear another's breath.

It's what strips your defenses, the dark a thick silence. And you think if only the sun would shine all night; if only there were no shadows, nothing to hide, your life flat and uncomplicated, a two dimensional painting. But all your needs are shades of black, creating depth, monstrous creatures, nameless and misshapen. You turn on all the lights in the house, adjust them so as you move from room to room, you don't cast shadows. And when you go to bed, take sleeping pills, turn out the lights. Close all the doors leading to your bedroom, afraid that if you wake in the middle of the night, the open closet will be the narrow passageway to a subterranean nightmare; your clothes bleached skeletons.

It's the distance between your lover's words and actions. A fault line you monitor for months until you can predict illusions.

You learn to trust the balance of assents/denials, intimacies/exclusions. Each time he calls, a seismic meter sounds inside your head and you brace yourself for the abrupt shift, the wall he erects, a cool hardening advancing in your bed. But silence, too, is a trust, a construction of space you inhabit, thicker than words he says when he's safe, separated by the width of a continent. And you wonder if his is a calculated risk your own destructive urge leads you to follow to a volcanic shore, to the smash of waves against cliffs and jagged reefs. But you believe beneath his crust, a melting point, and drift into its centre while he resists, equivocates.

It's what engulfs you later, as you drown in the arc of a stranger's arms, imagining your lover's hands, his mouth against your skin. Safe haven, soundless. Your mind begins a slow swim to the middle of the bay while water penetrates your mask, and breath is a yield to the depth. And in that moment when your lungs are exploding, your arms outstretched, you suddenly understand the distance, the danger, his coastline a receding horizon.

It's what you hear when your ex-husband calls from a pay
phone in Phoenix, Arizona, his tongue thick with liquor, to tell
you he is lonely. His words tunnel to a familiar room swelled with
new faces, while he, a spectre, hovers in darkened corners. His skin
dusk as wooden walls, his eyes the flare of a match struck in the
pitch of night. And you wonder what he expects — a miracle,
perhaps, a resurrection or a death. His voice weaves in and out,
past and present, muffled by passing trucks, woollen clothes, car
horns, tears. You listen to the noise it makes inside your head.
White noise. A synthesizer mimicking anger. And wonder why he
can't hear the sound of the word "no" pressed between you each
and every time he penetrates your dreams which are black and
white and sound like feet running, chasing or being pursued down
slick alleys and around corners that lead to grey metal stairways in
bad Hollywood movies when the heroine always climbs to the
roof and cowers, flat against a heating duct, listening to the
rhythmic beat of boots on rungs, insistent as the ring of the
telephone through which he follows you into your house, your
room, your head.

It's what you hear when your ex-husband calls from a pay
phone to tell you he is lonely: the thick silence of frozen streams,
dust and a sierra sunset slashing the sky.

It's how you love, soundless, like earth and darkness. Your lover whispers in your ear the need for words, the clear distinction of his name, a validation that you and he are here and present now. But you are versed in fear, in the hush when sleep begins and your breath quickens to the sound of scurrying in your dreams. Nocturnal creatures, like secrets, emerging unexpected. And you know they can claw a hole large enough for one evening when you were thirteen. A visit to a friend's house, comforting words. Then suddenly, the urge to run, though his arms hold you. Later, discomforting words: constructed remorse; your shame a destructive retort. And it's his betrayal that penetrates you more than his body, while you invent excuses. And tell no one.

It's how you live, later, in a house infested with rats only you can see. They nest inside you, burrow and screech along your spine. And your father, your mother, your sister, your brother ask what's wrong. But you only smile, disguise the rising revulsion, though each night, the rats crawl out and wander into your dreams, dark and uncontrollable.

It's what haunts you now, when your lover pleads with you to speak. And you do, only soundless, your love, a construction/destruction of words.

It's what you find when you re-enter your parents' house, years after you left. Your father's presence lingers in the half-filled cup, the open book, the grey worn cardigan which hangs, limp, on a chair back. He could be out for a stroll, or writing in his study while your mother lies, sedated, in their room, and cries. Disturbing sounds, each sob punctuating a series of endings which spring, unwanted, from within. Concertos for four hands, your parts slow, unrehearsed. And you recall your father sitting in the passenger seat of your car, applying pressure to a non-existent brake pedal while you accelerated the distance between you. Pursuing private visions or nightmares, escaping like he did, perhaps, years before, searching in oyster beds, prying shell after shell to uncover precious pearls. You recognize the symptoms, the flights, cause and effect. He led, you followed. The similarities knotted between you, held you in place. With each ending, a new beginning, or perhaps only the old reprised, a game whose rules you never knew any more than the stranger you discover in the funeral parlour when you pry open the lid.

It's what your mother captures when she leans into him and snaps a Polaroid photo. A gesture so final, you grab the camera and smash it against the casket, leaving welts in the redwood, while she stands to one side, holding the Polaroid negative which keeps developing even as he lies there. And when she peels back the black membrane, you try to recall his smile, his voice, the things which held you together — strings or fuses, or simply love or breath. A stony crescendo of things you could have said or done, but never did. And you press your foot on that non-existent pedal, braking the past again and again, seconds before you hear the siren of an ambulance late at night, the strident warning that here life clings.

A MATTER OF GENES

It's a matter of genes, your mother tells you. Your father has given you his errant eyes. How she hates the distance in those eyes — enough to travel twice around the earth — and now you rove. It's a matter of genes.

You ask her who invented the dream?

I'm earthly, your mother says. Your father has never felt the soil familiar; never stood still long enough for mud to cake him aground. He stands on flooding river banks, the rapids of his blood as dangerous as yours. But you know your mother has always been airborne. Your house has no walls, only day windows to split the sun in two, and night mirrors to record each restless move. She batters herself against panes, like a hummingbird cradled in pebbles on the outside. You have never seen the colour of her wings, only the motion. She will not talk about her past. This is a matter of genes, she insists, your father's. Always following a comet's wake and you, swallowing diamond dust, will suffocate like him.

But you have watched your mother perched on the black-hole edge; have seen your father's colours are illusions. Love is the flicker of black on white, a negative exposed to too much light. You search, dissatisfied; your ghosts, effects of the untrained eye.

Their genes built the airy cage they call their daughter or maybe you have winged their heels. This matter of genes could be retroactive — yours have determined their directions.

With heart attacks, your father cinches you into the houndstooth of his heart; with heart attacks, he distances you. Your mother paints oceans, knowing he can't swim. With heart attacks, he restrains you. *Don't cry*, he says. *Don't give me a heart attack.*

Don't, a dormant caustic substance implodes in action behind the curtains of your eyes. Ifs and whens. Now and then, fragments spill out, your father shouts, clutches his chest.

You welcome heart attacks, rage/love flip sides of a stone. Violent silence.

After the time his seed, like particles of snow, solidified, you grew. Your mother's tongue, thick with silken threads, spun a cocoon and bound you in your daughterhood. At night the dew dripped through the fine-spun strands. You saw her embedded in embroidery. But father wiped you off his knee like the last crumb emptied from his platter. You watched her careful eyes, felt warning fingered on your forearm. Fathers are fathers, not men, your mother's silence said. In folded darkness sheets, a shivering nightdress crumpled by your feet, your father spoke the language of snow. Through open curtains, you watched the flakes, heard them become one with pique, earthen lace.

Years later, you met for lunch and spoke woman to woman. You told of lovers trapped in cabin walls and logs of breathed-on heat. Married, you said, his wife was snow which beat upon the roof. You gathered her up at dawn with reddened fingers, and made tea. She laughed, your mother, not mother, not rival, accomplice to the games played on others.

Long after he was gone, you searched for him, dissected men but found no icy trace; loved only the remote in them, the maze. Your mother came for comfort. You donned the cape of words, grieved her lover, your disillusion cradled in a winter's grave.

There is no blizzard with the strength to separate your roles; now you are face to face, woman to woman, rival to rival. She melts a generation; takes your single state.

The key weighs heavy. Your mother's throat still white,
unmarked, though fingers pry, the trunk locked from inside.
You ask your mother to tell you lies, those things you've come
to believe. In her attic, ghosts assume bodies to haunt you both.
You want the story of their youths.

Your father had stars on his chest; she was a mermaid he
seduced to shore; he was a white ash, and she a cherry blossom
he held between his teeth.

Now tell me the truth, you say.

She strokes her throat. You would not want to hear it, she
replies.

Your mother smiles. You cup your hands to catch powder
falling from the corners of her clay mouth. Are the lights too
bright? She chose this stage, the thick curtains with no parting.
She has always wanted the centre, allowing you to take passive
roles, extras in the one-woman show. And now, she's tired, bored.
But you were never trained to take her place; to hear the roar of
lions, her admirers. In her arena, beasts stalk the inner passages
beneath her heart. She has starved them impatient with lies; has
made them ready to devour her.

Now you return, the daughter she has turned black and white in her darkroom. You came to resemble her, differences airbrushed by years apart. Now you return in full colour. She tries to expose your negative, burning in, dodging areas of subtle shades. You have developed in full sunlight, the contrast too marked to touch up.

You've always aged differently. While you moulted skin after skin, your mother wore hers in. You envied her, so well-fitted, while you shed a trail — lovers, ideas — none substantial enough to scale. Those transparencies have become melted by suns, brittled by ice, colours faded, brightness dimmed. Later, you tried her on: opaque and rigid, she would not take your mold. You continue to age, your recent skin sets, toughens new folds. Now you pick up after her as she sheds scale by scale. You examine each double-edge. Keep heirlooms. Fool's gold.

THE
HUNT

AURAL DEXTERITY

mother said don't love men
and they will

you have become ambivalent as song
and yield two separate sounds:

lyrics precise with reason
metre   balance   rhyme
wrought spontaneity
the timbre of the word *no*
a small steel hammer
losing its edge in the echo
of a battered heart

melody breathes
a dark eccentric storm
between bass drum beats
and guitar licks
jagged as cut metal
tense as the suspension
of desire

to fall in love
you need only
position yourself perfectly

between two speakers

TARGET PRACTICE

Don't shoot
until you see the whites of their eyes

eye contact
while making love

On the horizon
men are hardboard silhouettes

and you can almost shoot straight
though your arm is unsteady
from the butt's repeated kicks
your shoulder bruised

like that of a farm woman
nestling a rabbit in her arms
her hand strokes the head
later, one blow of the hammer
same hand, different motion
splits the skull

the heart
a swallow battered against ribcage

one night it soars
on the sighs between words
you chase it through streets
search it in lovers' beds
watch it land
into the outstretched hand
of a strange, familiar man

your father, perhaps
whose fingers
(same hand, different motion)
crush with delicate touch

AMBUSH

The alarm rings, or maybe it's the warning signal at a railway crossing, when the conductor sees a doe up ahead, eyes wide and hypnotized in the brilliant blizzard of light. You lie in bed, mesmerized by a dream in which your lover finally speaks a language you understand. And when you cloister to the surface, it's not the news you hear, but the lack of news. And this confuses you more than declarations of war, crimes of passion, stealthy intruders through basement windows and sliding doors. You push the covers back, slip on the blue kimono he slid off your shoulders those mornings behind closed shutters which let a pin of sun escape, like your eyes and his eyes. And when you reach the hall, and climb the darkened stairs, the moon carves windows on your walls through which you see him beckoning from a swatch of forest in the middle of a city. He glimpses your past, or your future, perhaps, or his own fear of involvement. And when he leans closer, urging you back, the leghold snaps.

SAFE PASSAGE

It's what expands when you seal your heart: external/internal infinite fear. Border crossings. You are quick, clutching your passport stamped with commitments; no private moments, no space to reflect, no room for another. Safe passage guaranteed. Don't look. The tortoise is advancing week to week, month to month. Later, you think, the future will be different. And you don't recognize it in your hurry, in your soporific frenzy for more work, more activities. Devour your life and everything will be right. Won't it? Because you know that those near you can see the tender regions between ribs, can aim. But the alternative is worse. You trust and expose.

It's the responses, need synonymous with fear. Silence is a thickness you wade through, a darkness you brave unable to sleep though you want to close your eyes and never reawaken, not till every emotion has shrunk into its shell. Black draws into itself the colours of the rainbow. You wait for that exquisite moment when the night sky slowly transforms from black to purple hues. Pace, helpless, through your house and touch absence. Everything here reminds you.

NEED

What need lures you to this masochistic place, where your stomach fluids churn; where you pace back and forth and in circles like a ridiculous figure in an old movie; where you fill every moment with activities because if you stop, you'll spiral into the depths of a hell even Dante couldn't fathom. Past the Ninth Circle. Deeper than thirteen. Where pain is numbing; you won't even be able to scream, or cry. You'll just die, maybe. But this is highly unlikely.

Sometimes you wonder if you are making it all up. If there isn't any place like this. If you create the hell, the well, something to drink from, something to climb out of; a passing updown lowhigh; how many ways can you badgoodfeel? How many ways can your lover make you (un)important, (in)secure — the ins and uns of love(rs) that make you feel you are somehow there for the taking, sometime when he feels like it, someplace where he doesn't want to be, someone he forgets easily, more easily than forgetting cigarettes when quitting smoking and he does quit and forget.

It's in the things he does, or in what he doesn't do, like tell you he'll see you tonight and not come; like go away for a week and not call, and act surprised if you act surprised. Hey what is this? A competition? Let's see who can be most surprised by who can do what to whom the most, the quickest, the longest, the hurtest.

So you think if it's not him then it must be you, something you're doing, something you want, you expect, you need. A sacrificial demand. You tell him he is inconsiderate. There. A nasty in-word. He is threatened. He is angry. He is wounded. Your words, he tells you with his silence, are stilettos in his heart. How could you possibly even think the unthinkeable?

But you do, and not only that, you say it too. Mostly because you're tired of blaming yourself for things he (un)does to make you feel the way you do. And you're tired of inventing threadbare (re)solutions, (de)fences — things to give yourself reason to see him again later, tomorrow, next week, forever, when all you want from him is need.

MATING IN
CAPTIVITY

DEAD MAIL

There are mornings you lie still
in the first stir of robins,
the chinking of a home,
dried grass and pine cones.

In your head, a clawing for order, husbands
lovers on microfilm, the alphabetical rendering
of your selves, parchment
peeled off the bark of an ash tree.

You've spread yourself so thin,
a few words here and there men never heard,
nor listened to; the flutter of wings
against a windowpane, sucked-in breath
and a door left unlocked.
You've always stood
in the palm of thunder,
in the wavering breath of lightning
splitting open a heart.

He comes to you in dreams, silent
as a pillow muffling the throat, intoxicating
as the scent of fireweed and bodies in August.

There are too many layers;
you choose the easy way — a deaf-mute.
You need only close your eyes to his echoes.

CONSTRUCTIONS

You sit in an architect's apartment. He is not your lover yet, because you have not shared your memories — the context which sets you apart. You invent each other a hundred different ways. Across town, your husband is waiting. You think about equality, choices, alignment. About split loyalties and betrayals, travelling between solitudes like the protagonist in a long-run play on Broadway. The curtain parts; men's roles reprise against rotating backdrops. Same script, only the gestures differ, the subtle inflection of the voice. Across town, your husband is waiting. Here, this man who is not your lover hands you a glass, a transparent offering, and explains the process of his work: to design a hotel complex in an area which man has not inhabited. He must create a story, a history from which his design can arise. One that progresses from the past (even if it is invented), lives in the present, and looks to the future.

You are the first to touch him. He must realize you come to him by choice, not by persuasion. And fall in love with him because he is willing to suspend credulity, because he doesn't need facts, because he offers such possibilities.

MATING IN CAPTIVITY

You're good at miming love
the thin distance
between the heart's murmur
and the hands;
time, a black space
flattened against white gloves.

Your feet have learned
to dance "I love you."
Constrained in toe-shoes
you glide
your half of a pas-de-deux.

"I need a family," he says
arid, cerebral

"Children cement a marriage."

You poise on either side,
silence, a fault line.

The stained walls
are tattoos of love
naked arms, moist eyes
an accidental brushing of elbows.

How to part your legs
and straddle the gulf?

He endeavours to teach the rule
"It's *natural* to have children."

Mother nature, *Mother* land
Mother tongue, *Mother* earth
Mother hood

But there are no rules
only secrets
pass the umbilical cord;

you feel the echo
of his mother's whisper
the link which binds you
belly to belly
with another mother's son.

Are you then destined
to yield your womb
to fit the traces
like a jigsaw

when in the end
his hair, his eyes
grow in your belly?

If only you could be
a nucleus.

You lie in the shade of his sleep
curtains spread
and the cool hand of the moon
strokes his lips, your heart
so easy to slide into his breath
easy as snow melts
as habits become

his yearning implodes
a TV image
his envy erodes
man and woman
husband and wife

you lie in the ache of his heart
the air, mellifluous
the sky, a black stone you must scale
to touch distant scars.

To kindle you
he scours your womb;
your mouth, a crescent moon
in a mackerel sky.

To make fire, to lure the iris,
in the legend
the boy tears a milk-white shell
from his chest;

to pierce the raven mouth,
in the legend
the boy wraps cedar bark
round arrowhead and bow.

Five years he stalks you
searching between drawn lips
arrowhead poised
searching behind the curtain of your lids.

He wears hunger
at the edge of his eyes
at the edge of his faltering desire.

And when he strokes your belly
five fingers, a palm
stretch across an expanse
of unsaid words
to shape a python
cinching the heart.

Honesty is a deep exhaling
a surrender
to the inevitable constriction.

"I'll have a family," he shouts
in the distance.

REVIVALS

He picks fireweed in summer
to blaze in a jar
the wild in them dies

in winter, buys tulips
bulbs buried in ice
to force fragile blooms

and later, in spring
locks ghosts in letters
and mails them to you

ESCAPE DREAMS

ESCAPE DREAMS

You live in a small apartment building; four or five floors, yours at the top. To see your apartment building, to make sure it really exists, you must climb the hillside opposite. From here, the city stretches brown and dusty to the foothills on the distant horizon. In the foreground, a row of shops extend and, to the left of these, your apartment building is attached, ominous and tall — a sentinel overlooking the flat tarred roof.

Often, when you lose your way, you return to this hillside, to remind yourself where you live.

Tonight, you are at a large party with your lover. In mid-conversation, words suddenly take prism shapes, disconnect themselves from sentences and float around you, like motes in sunlight. You think it is because you've forgotten something — context, language, your life, perhaps. You leave the party, certain that if you return home you will find whatever you have lost, though you don't recall any of the particulars, the hows and whens and whys. First, you return to the hillside to make sure your home exists, to find an entrance.

Each time, you take the same route: one flight of stairs, turn right; second flight, turn right; third flight, turn right. Your apartment is the first door on the right. Today, when you enter, you see a strange lobby extends in front of you into a narrow stairway. You climb, uncertain, and when you reach the landing, nothing is familiar. The walls are long curtains and the air is musky with incense. To the left is a second flight of stairs. You climb these too, and again, find yourself in unfamiliar surroundings. The hall, dark and musty, services four doors, none yours. You have stumbled into an enclosed apartment building within your apartment building.

You decide to retrace your steps, return to the hillside and find the proper entrance. However, when you descend to the first landing, it is unfamiliar once again. A narrow stairway leads down, and across from you, one leads up. You turn, and discover that the stairway you just descended has disappeared. From now on, no matter which stairway you take — up or down — you can never retrace your steps. Every movement, every turn is an act of magic, an invention of space.

You follow/create the stairs — snakes and ladders — until you reach the last landing, and step into the hall. One half of the floor is an apartment whose walls are made of glass. Thick curtains — gold snakes embossed in black — hang on the inside. You knock on the glass and wait until a man slides open an entrance. He is dishevelled, and smoking foreign cigarettes. You ask him directions to the exit. He shakes his head. You are here, he tells you. This is the beginning and the end. You turn toward the landing and see a wall where the stairs were. The man touches your elbow, flicking the ashes of his cigarette which disperse in the air before they reach the ground. He leads you to a door, says this apartment is empty and yours. You enter the large room and go to stand at the window from where you see the hillside. It is early evening, the sky a coral backdrop etched with the black silhouettes of foothills.

winter
angora snow
in front of you a large hill
you are sitting in a toboggan going up

Tropical landscape. Sunny and warm. The pavement is so white, foliage reflects in it. Monkey pods line the streets, make round fat shadows — umbrellas on a beach.

You are riding a tour bus, staring through tinted windows. You don't know who you are, where you've come from, or where you're going. In your hand, a ticket for a 4:30 train which departs from the lobby of a downtown hotel whose name you don't recognize. You get up and walk to the front of the bus, a little self-conscious because you don't know if you are young or old, pretty or ugly. You stare at your hands; smooth skin, scarlet fingernails, six gold rings. And men stare as you walk up the aisle, admiring glances, subtle proposals — this, at least, you recognize. You show the bus driver your ticket, but he shakes his head. You ask him to drop you along the highway, beside a tall gas-station sign. The gas station itself — the building and pumps — are gone. What is left is a large expanse of white cracked concrete in which grass grows in clumps. You cross this area, careful to avoid the cracks (break your mother's back), wondering who is your mother? and are you one? until you reach a green metal pole. Magically, a bus appears, and you board. When you show the driver your ticket, he too shakes his head. He will drop you at a different hotel where you can make a subway connection to the one you want.

When you arrive, it is a few minutes past 4:00. You walk through the main entrance, but can see no lobby. There is a long hallway onto which many doors open. You enter the first room, and find an amphitheatre filled with people listening to a young woman who is wearing a dark blue suit, a pillbox hat, and a white scarf tied at the throat. She could be a tour guide or an airline hostess. At the front of the room is another door. You go through it and discover an identical room to the one you just left. You pass through a series of identical doors, identical rooms and identical women. Finally, you ask one of the women to direct you to the lobby.

When you arrive there, it is 4:15, too late to make the connection to the train. You walk into a terrace coffee shop and sit down. The floor is white concrete, and lush plants and flowers are set all around the white iron-rod tables and chairs. In front of you are large concrete pillars and steps which lead down into terraced gardens and lawns.

A man stops by your table and asks if he can join you. And you let him, because he seems to know where you're going. He's catching the same train, he tells you, leading you by the hand into one of the amphitheatres, through the door up front into the next and the next and the next.

You have come to a foreign village because there is a man
here you want / don't want to see. You are constantly surrounded
by people, the man among them, but you avoid them all by
renting a space of your own for the afternoons. The building is
made of roughly hewn logs — blackened and weathered — and is
encircled by a wooden boardwalk which is constructed on six-foot
pylons. When you walk to the front entrance, your footsteps echo
in the empty space below. The main door is twelve feet high and
so heavy, you have to lean all your weight against it to open it.
Inside, you are alone. The ceiling is several stories high, and long
velvet curtains divide the room into sections. On the hardwood
floor are props, gymnasium equipment, and a series of ornately
carved trunks. One wall is mirrored and in front of it, extends a
dance bar. But you don't come here to dance; only to be silent
and alone. Each day when you leave, the man is waiting for you.
This is when you begin to dance, his eyes your mirror; your feet,
a resounding echo on wood.

And later, you find yourself at dinner. And this man who is/isn't your lover is sitting across from you. And there is blood on his white shirt. And there is blood on your hands.

Summer. Rural landscape. You are working at a summer lodge situated at the top of a hill, below which stretches an immense meadow. From your cabin, you reach the lodge by following a path through woods, then across the meadow. The path is narrow and in places, part sand, part dirt.

On the first day, when you set out toward the lodge, it is warm and silent. Only birds interrupt the stillness at irregular intervals. You walk, leisurely, until you reach a lakeside where people are bathing and laughing. You realize you must have taken a wrong turn. The meadow and the lodge are not visible. You backtrack, but no matter where you go, everything is unfamiliar. Finally, you reach a meadow, but you cannot see the hill or the lodge. In the distance, on the far left, is a farmhouse. But you are late and cannot go there to ask directions.

You continue to walk until the meadow ends abruptly at a ravine. Below you lies a city circled by a tall chain-link fence, like an immense power station. A thick silence pervades the air, makes you wary. Although you can see streets and houses and apartment buildings spaced at regular intervals, the city is immobile and inhuman.

You walk down the embankment, and along the perimeter of the fence until you find an opening. Once inside, you are on a main street which is four lanes wide and has a boardwalk up the middle. There are no cars, no people. Everything is white and hot.

Suddenly, a white car materializes at the curb ahead of you and a black woman gets out. She walks to a green metal pole and posts some letters. You approach her, to ask directions to the lodge, but before you can do so, she opens her purse and pulls out a poster. "You wouldn't be this person, would you?" she says, pointing to your name which is one of three on her poster. You nod. She laughs, folds the poster and puts it back in her purse. Then she begins to walk to the car. You follow her, insisting that you are who you are. Her smile lures you toward the waiting car.

And suddenly, you are afraid, and you run without looking back, run to the fence and along it until you find the opening.

You scramble up the embankment, across the meadow to the farmhouse in the distance. And as you approach, you see the house is missing an outside wall — like the doll house you had as a child. Inside, matchbox dressers, popsicle-stick tables and chairs, pin-cushion hassocks, and the walls lined in blue flocked silk — the remnants of one of your mother's sewing sprees. In the front room, two women squat on the floor, looking out. You ask them directions, and they point to a path which leads to the back of the house. The moment your feet touch the path, you find yourself in bed in your cabin, and it is the next morning and you recall nothing. You fall back into sleep and when you next wake, another day has passed. And so on, and so on.

You are lying prone in bed, dreaming/awake, watching through closed eyes a screen on which hovers a black creature, the size of your hand. You are afraid of this invention, this tangible secret which crawls along the wall. Your lover is in the shower; you hear the water running. You want to call to him for help, but he will not hear you.

You open your eyes and materialize a second creature adjacent to the first. This one is rectangular and two feet long. Down one side, it has a row of eyes; down the other, a row of legs, each a different colour: shades of reds, purples, browns, yellows. And suddenly, you are no longer afraid. You want to open the sliding glass doors and set them free. The water is still running. Your lover can't hear you. You close you eyes and feel the delicate weight of a spider's web settling over you, airy and beautiful. You fall asleep/awake and when you next open your eyes, you are looking between the black legs of a spider larger than your body. The water is still running. Your lover is still running.

You are lying, silent, in the arms of a man. Each time your mouths almost touch, you turn your head away, and long metal objects slither out between your lips. There are swords, knitting needles, stretched metal hangers, car parts. You remove them and set them between you on the bed.

Later, you push the covers back, slip on a blue kimono and go to a nightclub alone. There are many people here, sitting at tables, standing on chairs, leaning against the stage. You mingle among them, lean against the circular staircase in the centre of the room. Your lover appears at the top, carrying a vacuum cleaner. You watch as he descends and slowly begins to vacuum the colour out of the room. Everything turns to black & white. What astonishes you, is that the space between people is not empty, but a series of geometric designs with straight edges — diamonds, triangles, octagons. Bodies are delineated in black, but separate from the shapes between them. Sharpened knife blades.

DEPARTURES

lovErSCAPE

Your book falls open once again. You read and re-read the story, savouring gestures. His voice echoes the past, miles and miles of distance no technology can bridge. The page, an invention of space you inhabit together, untouched by the repetition of cycles. A black hole, perhaps, or the brilliant eye of a cyclone where you rediscover each other, while all around, the shattered remnants of your lives hurl past in a kaleidoscope of colour and texture. Unseen. Forgotten. An intuitive swell — how he spills into you, until you are no longer sure where you end and he begins. And you wonder if drowning is like this, the moment when air and water merge and the heart stops; or freezing, when the body welcomes the numb of frost and stops yearning.

Somewhere between the lines, you read the metaphors: husbands and lovers, fathers and sons, always leaving. You search the intimacy of a long moment, longer than phonecalls and hasty departures and arrivals. Longer than twenty years of running to and fro like a recurring flashback in a story, only it is the story and you won't admit it. And this, too, is part of those replayed scenes one of you always edits, while the other splices back on. And nothing is ever missing, except the present suspending you in one embrace.

RITUAL ENDINGS

Childhood sweethearts. She returns after a term at Oxford to kiss him goodbye; he shoots her in the act of leaving and turns the gun on himself. A photograph dropped in the rain the credits roll over — *MCMXCII All Rights Reserved* — like TV, when the film freezes her long legs frame by frame in the delicate slow-motion fall. Her head hits wood again and again, a diminishing replay, while up above he lies in a shadow of blood — testing boundaries — like TV, which grains the technicolour mass to black & white.

You walk the edge of the bay, balance on separate tracks of a railway skirting the ocean. A ritual undertaken at day's end, when the sun breathes the last goodbye. The hush of warmth clothes your words. Can it be that now, in the final lunge of parting, you are anaesthetized? The blade glistens from repeated thrusts, but you have seen too much blood on TV and don't recognize the quiver of stains.

DEPARTURES

Another house spent. The wood is old and winces with the remnants of three continents bulged in boxes. Your mother carries all the burdens from place to place. No house has seen her a decade.

Her boxes are filled with secrets, heirlooms you claim at each removal. Your teeth sink into the forgeries, discard the velvet-lined boxes with jewels shedding their lustre; diamonds which turn to crystals in the light. You are both strung like rosaries — each move yields one pearl; each departure knots years into place.

You became a family in Canada; four reeds skimmed off the crest of a rabid sea surging to this new shore. How did you know each other? Before you placed these roots, your father had tasted other seas, had smiled into the shutters of English cameras, English offices; had tasted other lands. Your mother strokes the tusks of an African adventure on the mantle; and the heavy bronze gong which you never struck except when home alone (your sister and you), afraid the ring would echo memories you hadn't shared, people you hadn't known; afraid he might heed the call. Who was he? you ask your mother, a question you never dared ask before, when he was still alive, when you could not tap into the hollows of his honeycomb.

Folded in quarters, the paper reads in English, with his Italian name neatly printed in centre. Your mother tells you he fought wars in offices with English writing behind his head and an IN-and-OUT tray, while you watched shadows lattice the ceiling of a bedroom in Bari, and wove his uniform of moonlight, coaxed stars onto the shoulders. He kept all the letters. Your words, childish, round with love, secreted in those hollows.

Before you became entrenched, your father followed a comet
with a quicksilver tail; followed it round each year to January 6th
when it led him to your door. He was a Maji, an echo of shoes on
stone. Morse code filling a gap larger than the space between you,
while you waited — white socks, white shoes — starched into a
dress since morning. He was the smell of fresh laundered uniform,
brass buttons, bottomless pockets emptied one treat at a time. The
mysterious gift-bearer who came seldom, who unburdened his
conscience with offerings. Lit candles inside you, made you
forgive the absence but never forget.

And after a day, a week, you'd feel the impatience of those
feet wanting to map new soils; and his eyes, blue with other skies.
(Later, you knew how he felt, when your own feet followed their
tapping. Divining, always divining. Always sure of this time, this
place, this man, as if all purpose were aimed at one experience
which continues to mutate, kaleidoscopic and erratic.)

For two years, you wrote letters to "*America*" your aunt said, ignoring borders, pointing to pictures of snow and igloos in the encyclopedia. Inside a church, your hand against cool marble, you imagined snow and Father — incongruous; he who made summers stretch, feet balanced on two hemispheres; he who loved colour and the shade of olive trees.

You came to expect the partings, the vigour of renewal. And in his absence, your lake waters calmed, waves licked the wounds until he, moon, split open a path.

Mother, wife, daughters, women with no power
to harness him. It took another,
an enchantress whose gifts he could not refuse:
        a tightening pearly necklace,
        the coolness of her hand.

Your mother went first, to melt the ice in him. You and your sister, frisky as ponies, shared a bed and dreams of slow-motion family pictures, until your aunt received the letter, cried till the words puddled together, then packed your clothes and took you to the waiting ship. Armed you with coloured paper and scissors to sever the ten-year bond. (Those ten years have taken root and turned melancholy into virtue; the monuments built inside your head grow taller, more erect in the shifting montage, the fragments of four choirs banded together to form a chamber.)

You became a family. You always thought your mother orchestrated melodies with a capricious hand, an avant-garde rendering of times and spaces, countries and cities superimposed at will. You learned to sing in different tongues: Sunday picnics, the four of you each settled in his score. Soprano, alto, tenor, bass. At times blended, harmonious; other times discordant. Your mother was conductor to charts written by your father's moods, sensitive to the dark *coloratura* of his nature, the comet no longer visible from this land.

In you, a continuity — your father's vision lasered on your retinas — *forever* and *always* have become finite in your dictionary. You wait for each death, each January 6th, each disillusion, for these are safe and familiar.

Though he lassoed his family
the enchantress returned,
brought milky clouds for his eyes,
*   silver threads for his hair.*
When he would not succumb, she retreated slowly
Later, returned, frequent, unexpected,
maimed him with molten lava for his blood,
*   and diamond locks for the valves in his heart.*

You became a family. In those short years, a son, the lineage
secure. Your mother has proof — the photos, loose in the large
envelope, shuffle themselves into a sequence of disruptions:

> a night at the opera. The conductor bows, lifts
> twenty years, supplants you in that other
> time when your father lowered the needle of
> the old gramophone onto the ebony disk,
> while you perched on elbows, legs raised and
> swinging, the libretto open to the first page

moved now as then, by the violin of death — Violetta's, your
mutual melancholy wish to be consumed in tragedy. Moved by
the vigour of his sadness, timeless and unmarred;

> communion dresses of soft white eyelet, and
> women with black hair, black eyes, black
> skirts. Hands clasped around rosaries,
> fingering their years, grounded in faith.
> Fingering the cool glass domes lined on
> dresser tops, passions remote as the saints
> inside; the morning of departure, a child
> nestled in the soft lap of the Black Widow
> married to god; nestled between the curtains
> pinned across unseen thighs, afraid of the
> dead groom hanging over her bed, two thorns
> plucked out by your sister to ease the pain

she waited patiently and this year joined the bridal train, her face
a fine net veil woven from 86 summer suns, her grey winter
filaments harnessed to a bun, amid flocked purple silk. You
imagine her withered body lithe with faith; arid and dusty as fields
after a long drought;

Italian summers. Your father struck through
a carbon ribbon two months a year, skin
blackened with sun. He spoke to them of
Atlantic shores, of jagged cliffs and the ocean
ripping open a seam, as he spoke to you of
fireflies, of figs picked fresh, of the great-
aunts' faces furrowed with mirth

he was a poet constructing an eulogistic monument, each word
sculpted out of the severing of his essential need, his amputated
homeland quivering an uncontrollable metre in his heart.

You became a family. Your mother and father spoke English
to you, their foreign daughters who became Canadian, determined
as reformed smokers, through fluency
    through the fairness of your skin
    through the straw and berries of your hair
    through the unspoken oath of allegiance renouncing all that
was not shared. Your house was built of one fabric, each of you
basted into his square. When fitted, it kept you warm for those
short years.

His enchantress returned one January 6th.
Unloosened the seams.
He did not scorn her impatient giving:
   the dance into her body,
   the bed of soft moist earth.

Another house spent. You have inherited your mother's fear of permanence. Your decades await the isolated bead of a Glory Be, necessary as a life-preserver. You renovate each house until it is too perfect to inhabit.

THE RETURN

After a generation, unshared intimacies, you return, a swallow scenting its birth-trail. Gingerly you tread the soil, hard-packed with death and tears of women, wearing your Canadian shoes like a protection against a contagious disease.

Your father's home lies in the midst of a fault split open by an earthquake and the clean slice of plane tickets; filled with the shard remains of promises, of hollow laughter and letters written from Canada. You search among the ruins: his joy, children's songs, evenings of fireflies and wine and grandfather telling stories. But they are buried under Lombardy poplars, among gravestones and women who wear pain like a cancer of the heart.

The air is charged with dust, fear, melancholy, superstition, an industrial disease seeping into the pores. You long for the tentacles of evergreens, for wind lying flat against a wheat stalk, for the splash of feet in either ocean; your distant land vivid as your father's dream of Italy. You have come to replant your feet and read your name in the marble slabs under which dust gathers your generations one inside the other.

Printed in Canada